Fionn Mac Cumhail's
Tales from Ireland

Eddie Lenihan

Illustrated by Alan Clarke

MERCIER PRESS

Cork

www.mercierpress.ie

© Text: Eddie Lenihan, 2015

Stories adapted from *Irish Tales of Mystery and Magic,*
published by Mercier Press in 2006.

© Illustrations: Alan Clarke

Produced for Mercier Press by Teapot Press Ltd

Abridged and edited by Fiona Biggs
Designed by Alyssa Peacock & Tony Potter

ISBN: 978-1-78117-357-2

10 9 8 7 6 5 4 3 2 1

A CIP record for this title is available from the British Library

Printed and bound in China

CONTENTS

Fionn Mac Cumhail
and the
Feathers from China

A stranger appears at Tara, telling
a tale of a great way to conquer
your enemies – using feathers!
Fionn and the Fianna put it to the
test and use it to
make a chieftain
pay his taxes.

Long ago in Ireland, Fionn and other heroes had many adventures in faraway places. One of them, Maeldún, brought home strange stories about a land on the other side of the world called China, where everyone wrote backwards! But none of his stories was stranger than the one about how the Chinese used to punish people. Here is how the Fianna heard this story.

One night, there was a feast in the banqueting hall of Tara – but King Cormac was bored and sat with his head between his hands.

'Ohh! I've heard all the stories before, and I'm sick of it. If only someone had a new tale!'

At that, there was a loud knock on the front door.

'Open that, quick,' said the king, 'it might be a stranger with a new story.'

In strode a tall, sunburnt man.

'God save you, your highness,' he said.

'And who are you?' asked the king. 'If you have a story for us then you're our guest of honour!'

'Hah! Story, is it? That's the very thing I have, and a story the like of which no one here has ever heard!' said the stranger confidently.

'Aha! My prayers are answered,' said the king. 'Bring him a bite to eat, so he can begin his tale!' he ordered, and he settled down to enjoy the stranger's story.

When the last of the crockery had been cleared away the stranger settled back, looking slowly at the crowd from face to face and began:

'I was on a ship …' he said, puffing his pipe as he remembered, 'and where we went to … 'twas a place called China.'

'Ohh! Begor!' said the men. 'Where's that? Is it anywhere west of *Inis na Rón*?'

'No,' he said, 'it's the other direction entirely. I don't rightly know how we got there because 'twas dark most of the way and we slept a good deal of the time. The rest of it was lightning and thunder, and the wind was blowing us places we didn't want to go at all.'

'Hu-hoo!' cried the men of the Fianna, 'that's the only kind of a journey to go on, 'cos you'll always find interesting things when you're expecting nothing.'

'But come on,' said Conán impatiently, 'tell us about China.'

'Well, the people were small, with yellow skin, and they'd look at you fierce and strange. And they all had tails out of the back of their heads.'

'Oh, they sound weird! Would they bite you?' cried the listeners.

'No. But wait 'til I tell you. Didn't the women there dress like the men, and the men like the women!'

'Aghh!' cried the Fianna. 'That must be a terrible place, all right. But tell us more!'

'They had strange big animals with two humps on their backs, camels they called them, and we had to perch on one of the humps while the driver perched on the other one. Off we went, and it nearly crippled me.'

The men of Ireland had never heard anything about camels, so it made a big impression. Round the tables it went, from man to man, each one rolling the word up and down in his mouth as if he were sucking marbles.

'We travelled across
the land of China,' continued
the stranger, 'and the sun
would fry your brains
because there wasn't a stem
of greenery in the whole
place. There was only rock
and stones and sand.'

When men of the Fianna
heard that there were no
woods or chirping birds in
this hot, dry land, they
began to feel that this
was not the place for
them, even if they
could have seen it.

'We kept going for thirty solid days and nights,' said the stranger. 'At night there'd be icicles hanging off your nose, but in the morning 'twould be frying your skull again.

'At the end of thirty days, travelling every day full blast, we came to a wall, just like the wall of a *dún,* only bigger. There were towers all along it, and men guarding it, and on top of it wasn't there a road.'

'*A Thiarna milis!*' the men groaned. 'Worse and worse!'

'Well, we climbed onto the wall on a ladder – they even had a place for bringing up the camels – and off we went along the wall. We marched for thirty more days but the road went on and on … Up the sides of mountains it went, down into huge valleys, across great plains …

'We came at last to the sea, and there the road ended.'

Relief showed on every face.

'And there on the sea, stretching as far as our eyes could see, were ships, as many as a man could count in a year and a day.'

'What class of ships?' croaked Liagán Luaimneach.

'Square ships with pictures painted on their sails, and a little house like a small *dún* at the stern.'

'We drove the camels over a timber bridge and onto the ship nearest the shore. Then we rode the camels for three days over the decks of the ships, out and out to sea with never a stop. When we came to the last ship there was no trace of any land in front of us or around us, so we looked in the only other place there could be land, straight down, and sure enough, below us in the green water we saw a city, with people going about their business.

'The camels walked over the side of the last ship, one after the other, and made no attempt whatsoever to swim. I closed my eyes and said my prayers, thinking I was surely drowned. I held my breath, felt myself going down and down, and when my eyes popped open at last from the lack of air they nearly fell out of my head entirely when I saw where we were – safe and sound inside in a big bubble. Dry land under the sea.'

'What were the people like there?' asked the men.

'The same type as in the other place. But listen now,' said the stranger, ''cos 'tis here the interesting story starts,' he winked.

'Hold, now, for a minute!' said Cormac in a shocked voice, 'until we fill up the drinking-cups again. This is fierce thirsty work.'

After a pause, the stranger continued: 'We were brought to one of the wise men of the city and I asked him how did they keep the sea out and themselves in.'

' "Oh," he said, "we have the books of power." '

At this, the Fianna started whispering to each other, saying, 'Wouldn't it be handy if we had a place like that, to hide from our enemies. Faith, we'll have to ask Taoscán Mac Liath about it.'

Cormac shouted: 'Silence at once!'

Quietness fell, and the stranger described the type of houses and streets in the place.

Fionn felt that he had to put in a word. 'Tell me, used they fight there?'

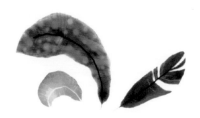

'No,' replied the stranger firmly. 'There was no fighting because everyone was too afraid.'

'Afraid! Of what?' Fionn was getting interested in this new mystery. He thought there might be lessons to be learned from the people of China that he could use when dealing with his enemies.

'Oh, they were frightened out of their wits of the fierce torture in that place.'

'Ahhh!' sighed Cormac. 'This is more like it. Tell us about it! Did you see any of it?'

'I did. It was so simple. I was let in when they were going over one of the enemies of the people in the torture chamber. You can imagine my shock when I heard this ferocious laughing and screeching coming from inside the prison.

'I said to myself, "That's a strange prison."
There were rows of big iron doors, and so much
laughing going on behind those doors that I
began to wonder was I in my right mind at all.
I picked out a door where the laughing seemed
louder than the rest, and knocked. Two big, bald,
burly men answered the door. There in front of
me was a man lying on a table, tied by his hands
and feet with leather straps.

'He stretched up his neck when he saw me and
there was terror in his eyes! He shouted out, then
the two big men went to work again.

'"Oh," I said to myself, "what kind of
weapons do they use, now, is it red hot irons?"

'One of the big men went around the other
side of the table and started flexing his huge arms.
He started humming to himself as he turned to
the wall.

'On a little shelf there was a row of feathers.
He put up his hand into the middle of the feathers
and took out one of them.

'The big man began at the soles of the poor
man's feet and started tickling him. Well, you'd
hear his screeching a mile away. And by the time
he got up to his oxters the breath was gone from
him and he was gasping for mercy. He was nearly
quenched from all the laughing! The other jailer,
who was standing by my side looking on at all this,
said, "That will do for now! Maybe our friend from
the western world has seen enough."

'They released the poor man and off he went,
shaking, half-laughing, half-crying to himself.
I asked, "Is that the way you deal with criminals
and hoodoos in this place?"

' "That's it," they said. "And by the time that man is done once, he's a model citizen for ever more! He won't be back again – you can be sure of that!" '

After that, the Fianna only wanted to hear about the feathers and how they were handled. Fionn and the stranger went out to the duck-house and when Fionn came back into the hall again he threw a mighty *gabháil* of feathers onto the king's table and the stranger began to sort the feathers. Cormac stared at the man's flying fingers.

'That one here, and this one there …'

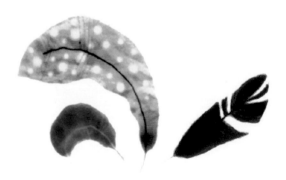

When he came to the smallest feather he called it
'the one that'll drive a man out through himself
with the laughing after cudgels might have been
hopping off of him for three days with no result. I
paid very careful attention in China to the different
feathers for different jobs. There's one for the sole
of the foot, one for behind the knee, one for under
the lug. There's no place that a feather can't be
found for.'

'I can't wait to try them out for myself,' said
Fionn. He picked out a feather. 'What's this one for?'

'That's for the top of the head,' the stranger said.

'Conán Maol! Come here!' ordered Fionn.

Conán made his way to the high table, his bald head shining in the torchlight.

He sat down, and Fionn started tickling his head with the feather. No effect.

'You're not doing it right,' said the stranger, 'watch me.' He gave a demonstration with the feather that left Conán ready to collapse.

King Cormac was beginning to see how useful the feathers could be. He said, 'I'm looking for someone to do a small job for me, and it might involve a bit of persuasion.' All the Fianna put up their hands.

'Good men! I knew I could rely on the Fianna,' he smiled. 'Here's what I want. Those Ó Flátharta blackguards in Connemara owe me a lot of tax. If you can make them pay I'll make these feathers part of the Fianna's standard equipment.'

'We'll do it!' shouted Fionn.

Next day Fionn and his men got their sets of feathers from the stranger and they set out for Connemara, leaving all their own weapons at Tara. A day later they arrived at the *dún* of Ó Flátharta Gorm. Fionn called out, 'Open the gate! We have a message from King Cormac, High King of Ireland!'

The gate was opened and when Ó Flátharta saw that the men had no weapons he said in his most friendly voice, 'Come in, come in!' He was highly amused when he saw the feathers around the waists of the Fianna.

Fionn said, 'King Cormac says that you owe him money, and if you won't pay we'll take it from your treasury.'

'You have no weapons,' scoffed Ó Flátharta.

'Tell him I'm not paying until he makes me do it.'

'I'd think a bit more about it, if I was you,' said Fionn. 'We're peaceful men, but if we're rubbed the wrong way … So look! If you give us the taxes, like a good man, there'll be no more noise.'

Ó Flátharta said he'd ram them all into his deepest dungeon and pour boiling gruel in on top of them if they didn't clear off back to Tara.

'All right,' said Fionn mildly. 'But you'll meet us again … shortly!' And he turned around and left with his men.

That night, while Ó Flátharta and his men celebrated the victory, the Fianna returned. They climbed through the window of Ó Flátharta's sleeping chamber and settled themselves in.

In the small hours of the morning Ó Flátharta threw open the door, collapsed into bed and was soon snoring. He woke up when a hairy hand sailed out of the darkness and clamped itself over his mouth.

Diarmaid lit a candle and set it beside the bed. The chief's eyes darted around the room and he thought his last hour had surely come.

Four of the men moved to the bed to hold Ó Flátharta down.

Keeping one hand over the chief's mouth Fionn picked the toe-feather out of his belt. He began at the toes and worked up, changing feathers every so often. After a short while Ó Flátharta was weak from laughing and his shrieks could be heard all around the *dún*.

By this time an excited crowd of Ó Flátharta's men had gathered in the corridor outside.

'Hi! Chief, chief! Are you all right?'

All he could say was 'Eeee-aaa-ah-ah-ahh!' They thought there must surely be evil spirits in the room with him, yet they didn't dare break down the door.

When Fionn had finished he opened the door and the guards rushed in, weapons drawn.

'Softly now,' mocked Fionn. 'Is it the custom in these parts to attack men with no weapons?'

That stopped them.

They looked at Ó Flátharta, who was just beginning to come back to himself. He was cringing in a corner of the bed, shaking, eating his fingers and whispering to himself in a strange language.

'He's bewitched,' said the guards.

'No,' thundered Fionn. 'That man was defeated with this' – holding up a feather. They all gaped. How could the mighty Ó Flátharta Gorm be defeated by a feather?

But they knew Fionn would not lie – no man in any of the four corners of Ireland could call him a liar. So they huddled, frightened, in the courtyard of the *dún*.

After a few minutes Fionn strolled out, followed by the other men of the Fianna.

The guards backed into a corner, looking for a way out up the walls, but then a scraping sound was heard from the direction of Ó Flátharta's chamber and out crept the man himself.

'Men,' said he, sobbing, 'get my money chest! Get it, quick. Ye know where it is!'

Three of his guards sprinted for it.

'Take it all,' he whimpered to Fionn. 'I'll pay ten years' tax now in advance. Only go away and take your cursed feathers with you.'

Ó Flátharta never told his men what had happened in his sleeping chamber that night, but the following day he went out alone and killed every bird in the *dún*. And ever afterwards, as long as he lived, no bird, tame or wild, was safe near the *dún* of *Indreabhán*. Word spread about these strange happenings at *Indreabhán* and as a result there was a huge improvement in law and order all over Ireland. All thanks to the feathers!

Fionn Mac Cumhail
and the
Making of the Burren

Everyone knows that the Burren is
a strange-looking place where no
crops grow. This is the amazing
story of how it was made by Fionn
and the Fianna, and why.

Long ago, there was a king in Clare who was known as Aengus the Generous. His door was open to everyone and he was famous from one end of the county to the other for his huge feasts. One thing he was very fond of was eels, cooked any way his chef might prepare them.

Aengus always looked forward to the May Day feast of eels, the first of the new season.

Now, at that time the only place where top quality eels could be got was Doolin.

As May Day approached all the preparations were being made as usual, when a messenger came staggering into the palace, his clothes hanging in rags about him.

'Your majesty!' he cried, when he was brought before the king. 'A terrible thing! Ballykinvarga fort is invaded by villains and they're saying that this year they won't let you bring any eels through their land if you don't pay them a sack full of the purest gold.'

'What!' cried Aengus, jumping up in a fury. 'No eels?'

'Oh, your majesty, they said they're sick and tired of letting you and all your people take advantage of them by crossing their lands, and not a morsel out of it. No gold, no eels, they said.'

'They won't get away with this,' shouted Aengus. 'Call for the Fianna!'

Fionn had arrived in Clare with twenty of the Fianna the day before, specially invited for the May feast. 'What are we going to do?' he asked his men.

'We'll get the eels!' they roared in reply.

'Start going, so,' said Aengus. 'You have only three days to get back here with the eels in time for the feast, otherwise there's going to be murder.'

The Fianna marched off and soon they were in the Burren, but the men of Ballykinvarga fort had laid a trap. They had balanced huge rocks on a hilltop, ready to roll at the slightest push. They rolled the big rocks down on top of Fionn and his men. The Fianna managed to jump out of the way only at the last minute.

They were just blowing the dust off themselves when a shower of arrows rained down on top of them. They raised their shields to make a roof for themselves.

'Come on!' shouted Fionn. 'Every man draw his sword and get up that hill!'

In the space of five minutes they were standing panting on top of the hill, but the ambushers had seen them coming and had skipped off.

'Now lads, look!' said Fionn. 'We'll have to be careful from here on because these boys are out to make things rough for us. We'll have to watch where we put our legs. There could be all kinds of traps set for us. But remember that we have less than three days to get the eels.'

They went on, but far more carefully than before. That night they made their camp near the stone fort of Caherconnell, but lit no fire in case their enemies might see the smoke. Anything they ate that night was eaten cold and swallowed with water.

The following morning, Fionn said, 'Now, men, today we'll get to the big stone fort of Ballykinvarga; there's no other way to Doolin but to pass opposite the gate. So here's what we'll do. I know that fort well, and I know it because I was in on the building of it. There's no way into the fort,' said he, 'except one small door.

'What we'll do is this,' he said.
'We'll make little of the fellows inside. We'll
call them cowards and warts and bandits.
But we'll keep well out of the way of their
spears and arrows. And when they have
all fired all their weapons at us, we'll
abuse their fathers and mothers and
grandfathers, and if that doesn't drive
them mad altogether I'm losing my
touch. It won't be long before they'll
be throwing the stones out of the wall
at us. And we know what the finish
of that'll be, don't we. So now, every
man think of as many bad names as
he can while we're marching.'

About five miles further on, a stone battlement loomed up in front of them. They stopped. 'Up to the fort with three of you!' said Fionn, 'and give them the message from King Aengus.'

Conán advanced with two men. He shouted out, 'Men inside the fort there! I want a word with the leader.'

A large ugly head rose up slowly above the wall. "*Dar an leabhar!*" cried Conán, 'look who it is!'

'Who is he?' asked his companions.

'It's Leathshúil himself.' Conán knew this ruffian well.

Out of the corner of his mouth Conán said to his two companions, 'Lads, there's going to be things flying here in a couple of minutes so be ready to move. I know this boyo and he's a bad case.'

But he said to Leathshúil in a calm voice, 'Step aside and let us pass, or there'll be trouble.'

In reply Leathshúil gave an evil laugh, and
a shower of arrows sliced through the air, but
the three Fianna were already on their way
back to their companions. Fionn gathered the
men around him and said, 'Remember the plan.
Out now, and make them fire all their arrows.'

Out they trooped, but not too close to the
fort. The men on the battlements fired showers of
arrows at them, only realising too late that they
had run out of ammunition!

'Ha-hah!' laughed Fionn. 'The second part
of the plan, men. Now!'

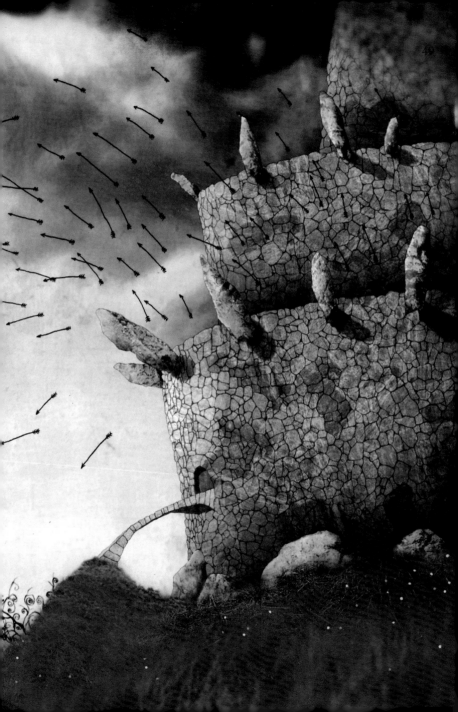

All together, they jumped forward, nearer to the fort, put down their spears and shields and started making faces and letting out the most fierce and horrible jeers.

Nobody inside the fort made any move. To get things going, the Fianna fired a few boulders and one hit Leathshúil on the head. He ordered his men to fling rocks back at the Fianna and so the battle started in earnest. With Leathshúil in command the men inside were soon giving as good as they got so that the Fianna had to move back. Soon they were scattering in every direction, looking for boulders of all sizes to fling at their enemies. On and on it went, until night came on a second day. As far as the eye could see the landscape was all rooted up because the Fianna were having to travel further and burrow deeper in order to find suitable ammunition. What a strange, moon-like landscape it was by the time they finished their day's fighting.

The next day, the battle went on, pounding, pelting, fighting and tearing, with rocks flying in all directions. But the Fianna were growing tired and Fionn could see they were going to lose the battle if something was not done quickly.

He reached his hand into his bag and pulled out a small bottle. He poured a drop from it onto the back of his hand and hairs sprouted from his wrist. He told everyone to take a drink from the bottle and they were soon jumping out of their skins with energy, mad for any kind of action.

'I want that fort buried by the time I am finished smoking my pipe!' shouted Fionn. He need not have worried as Ballykinvarga had vanished in a cloud of dust long before that.

The Fianna set off for Doolin, and when they arrived they found the eels all loaded up and ready, packed in big timber kegs. But it turned out that the horses that were meant to pull the big carts laden with the barrels had been stolen the night before.

'We have less than a day to get this cargo back to Aengus,' said Fionn. 'There's nothing else for it but to pull these carts ourselves.'

They set out at a great pace, making the road fly under them, and people rushed out of their houses along the way to see the sight. The Rás Tailteann was nothing compared to it. Sweat flowed off them as freely as Torc Waterfall, spattering the spectators standing at the side of the road.

It was dark by the time they were getting close to Aengus' fort, and Aengus was on the battlements, stamping over and back, over and back, with his bad temper written all over his face.

'Where are my eels? Where are my
eels?' he snarled.

Then one of the guards ran up,
breathless, and wheezed, 'Your majesty,
there's noise coming from the road.
Would it be your eels, do you think?'

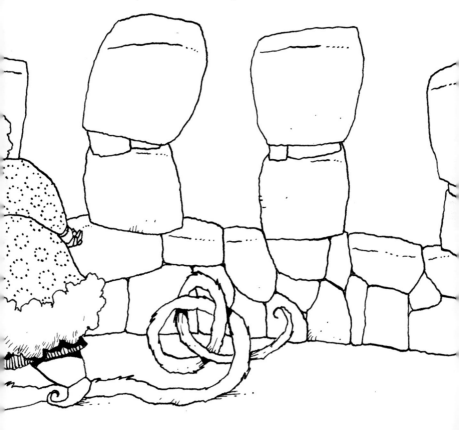

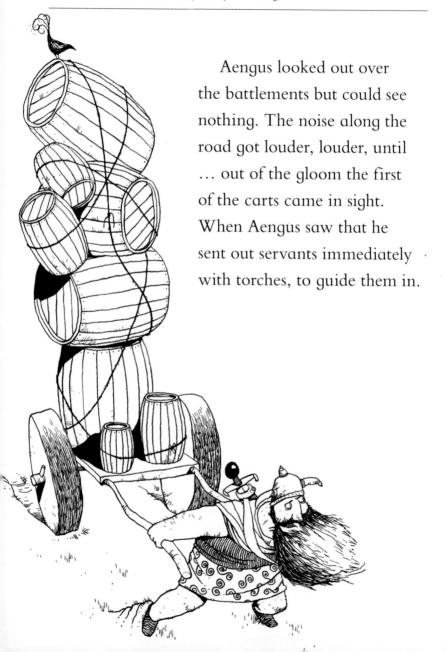

Aengus looked out over the battlements but could see nothing. The noise along the road got louder, louder, until … out of the gloom the first of the carts came in sight. When Aengus saw that he sent out servants immediately with torches, to guide them in.

When he saw who was under the shafts of the carts, that there were no horses there at all, he burst out into big *scairts* of laughter.

Fionn didn't see what was so funny, but he was only too accustomed to kings and their little jokes so he said nothing. The men under the carts had nothing to say either; they were completely exhausted and bathed in a lather of sweat.

All they could do was lie down in a corner and fall asleep immediately.

Now the cooks took charge of the barrels and carried the eels to the kitchens. They fried, boiled, toasted, roasted and frittered; they made pastes and pastries and all kinds of pies. Everything was ready on time. When the guests surged into the feasting-hall not one of them could have guessed what trouble those eels had caused. But the problems were not half over, though no one yet knew that.

The feast went off beautifully, of course, but none of the Fianna was there to enjoy it except Fionn, who had carried the sleeping Fianna to bed, one by one, and had left them all lying in the one big bed, sound asleep. There they lay now, and for three days afterwards, dead to the world and shaking the walls with their snoring.

For three days after the feast not a sound – except the snoring of those men upstairs – was to be heard around the fort, not even a dog scratching himself. Every living creature inside was asleep, dreaming about eels and next year's feast.

Then, early on the morning of the fourth day a mob of people gathered at the front gate of the palace and began a fierce hullabaloo. They woke everyone inside with their banging and shouting, even King Aengus, who staggered out.

When they saw him they shouted, 'We're from the Burren! The Fianna destroyed our land; they rooted it all up!'

'They did?' returned Aengus. 'I heard nothing about it if they did. You're talking *ráiméis* and I'd advise you to go home, at once.'

But there was no quietening that crowd, so Fionn was summoned to the royal presence.

'What's this I hear from that gang out there? They're saying you ruined the land on them, that 'tis only full of stones and rocks now, as well as big holes. Is that true?'

'We had to do a bit of rooting and tunnelling all right to – ah – kind of quieten the crowd inside in Ballykinvarga fort.'

'Well, well!' said Aengus. 'This could be very expensive. I have no money to be throwing into holes in the Burren at this moment. Root up your men out of the bed and tell them there's a small bit of a job in front of them.'

Aengus strolled back to the farmers and announced, 'Look! Fionn Mac Cumhail and the Fianna will be up tomorrow to fix up any damage. That's the best I can do for you.'

They had to take his word for it and go home. Aengus went back to bed.

Later that day Fionn and the men started out. When they reached Ballykinvarga fort they listened closely, but could hear nothing. They began to take the rocks that they had thrown in on top of the fort and hurl them out in every direction, out around the countryside until the fort could be seen again.

The farmers, though, were furious when they saw the new state of their land. 'Aaaa! Yeee! Blast it, sure it's useless now. There's no soil at all, only a solid sheet of rock.'

Back they went to Aengus again, an evil-tempered mob, armed with pikes and other weapons. Aengus came out on the balcony.

'Get out of here at once, or I'll set the dogs and the Fianna on you. You weren't satisfied the first time and now, when the job is done right, you aren't satisfied either. So off with you!'

What else could they do but slink away? Eventually they had to leave that part of Clare because they could get no living from the land. Anyone who looks at the Burren today will understand why, for it still looks just the way the Fianna left it all those centuries ago.

Pronunciation guide

A Thiarna milis – a hear na millish (O sweet Lord)

Conán Maol – cunnawn mweel

Cormac – core mack

Dar an Leabhar – darr on lower (by the book/Bible)

Diarmaid– dearmwid

Dún – doon (fort)

Fianna – feeanna

Fionn Mac Cumhail – finn mack cool

Gabháil – gahwall (armloads)

Indreabhán – indra wawn

Inis na Rón – inish na rone

Leathshúil – lah hool

Liagán Luaimneach – lee agawn looimnock

Maeldún – mwale doon

Ó Flátharta Gorm – oh flaharta gurrum

Ráiméis – raw maysh (nonsense)

Rás Tailteann – rawse tahltan

Scairt – skahrt (guffaw)

Taoscán Mac Liath – tayscawn mack leeah